The Skipping-Rope Snake

For Ella, with love from Mummy – C.D.

For Sheffield – L.M.

First published in 2003 by Macmillan Children's Books
A division of Macmillan Publishers Limited
20 New Wharf Road, London N1 9RR
Basingstoke and Oxford
Associated companies throughout the world
www.panmacmillan.com

ISBN 0 333 99327 6

nesta

Carol Ann Duffy gratefully acknowledges a Fellowship from NESTA.
NESTA – the National Endowment for Science, Technology and the Arts –
was set up in 1998 to support innovation and creative potential in the UK.

The Skipping-Rope Snake

CAROL ANN DUFFY

illustrated by LYDIA MONKS

MACMILLAN CHILDREN'S BOOKS

The snake in the jungle
spoke with a lisp,

hung from a branch, like a limp wrist,

slithered

    hither and thither,

      hissed,

        slid out its fangs,

         whispering,

"Kith?"

to the lions
and the tigers
and the hippopotamus.

The snake in the jungle snoozed in the dust,
opened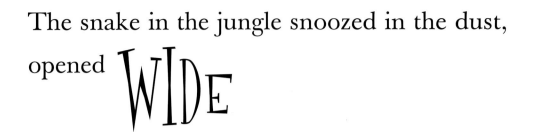

when a mouse squeaked past,

squeezed like a vice
    if it got the chance
to cuddle up to monkeys
    or orang-utans.

To Jungle

A little girl came walking in the jungle one day,

looking high and low
for a game to play.

She tried Join-the-Dots
on a leopard's spots,
but her pencil jabbed
and the cat got cross.

She tried playing

SNAP!

with a
crocodile,

but it just couldn't shuffle
and she didn't like its smile.

She tried playing Pin-the-Tail
on an elephant,

but she poked her pin –

OUCH!

– into its trunk.

Then just when she was thinking
coming here was a mistake,

she saw

coiled on the ground

a skipping-rope snake.

Quick as a parrot-squawk,
she tied two knots –

one at its end

and one at its top –

then she skipped away
out of the jungle,

homeward-bound,
singing a jingle:

"Skipping home is a piece of cake

when you've got your very own skipping-rope snake."

The snake was horrified,
cross-eyed,
tongue-tied.
Swished in the air with a *whoosh*
like a whip!
Flicked on the ground with a *skoosh*
like a skip!

But the girl

and the skipping-rope snake

skipped fast –

bye-bye, rhino,

bye-bye, giraffe,

bye-bye, gorilla,

bye-bye, bats,

bye-bye, lemurs,

bye-bye, big cats –

"I'm off home,
make no mistake.
I've got my very own
skipping-rope snake!"

That night,
the little girl slept in her bed,
jungly pictures
filled her head –

glowing tigers
the colour
of carrots,

turquoise hummingbirds,

firework parrots,

blackboard panthers

with chalk-white teeth,

a swinging washing-line

of chimpanzees –

and the snake in the playroom
hung
from a hook,

next to a teddy
and a fairytale book,
dreaming of the jungle,
talking in its kip . . .

'Fangs for the memory,'

skip,

skip,

skip."

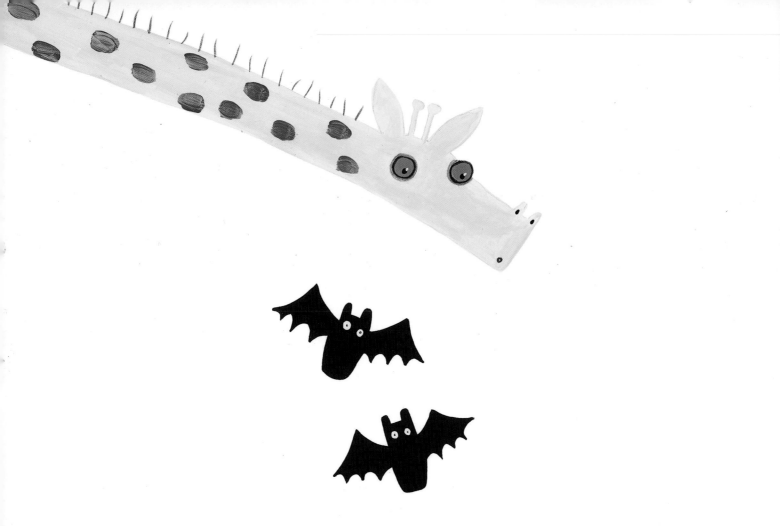

If you have enjoyed reading this book,
why not try *Queen Munch and Queen Nibble*
also by Carol Ann Duffy and Lydia Monks.